✗ Captain Dom's Treasure ✗

Don't miss the other books in the Definitely Dominguita series!

#1: *Knight of the Cape*

Coming soon:
#3: *All for One*

Definitely
DOMINGUITA
✖ Captain Dom's Treasure ✖

By
Terry Catasús Jennings

Illustrated by
Fátima Anaya

ALADDIN
New York London Toronto Sydney New Delhi

ALADDIN

An imprint of Simon & Schuster Children's Publishing Division
1230 Avenue of the Americas, New York, New York 10020
First Aladdin hardcover edition March 2021
Text copyright © 2021 by Terry Catasús Jennings
Illustrations copyright © 2021 by Fátima Anaya
Also available in an Aladdin paperback edition.
All rights reserved, including the right of reproduction in whole or in part in any form.
ALADDIN and related logo are registered trademarks of Simon & Schuster, Inc.
For information about special discounts for bulk purchases, please contact
Simon & Schuster Special Sales at 1-866-506-1949 or business@simonandschuster.com.
The Simon & Schuster Speakers Bureau can bring authors to your live event. For more
information or to book an event contact the Simon & Schuster Speakers Bureau
at 1-866-248-3049 or visit our website at www.simonspeakers.com.
Book designed by Heather Palisi
The illustrations for this book were rendered digitally.
The text of this book was set in Candida.
Manufactured in the United States of America 0121 FFG
2 4 6 8 10 9 7 5 3 1
Library of Congress Control Number 2020948864
ISBN 9781534465060 (hc)
ISBN 9781534465053 (pbk)
ISBN 9781534465077 (ebook)

To Terina, who taught me to read, and to Rafael,
who taught me to love books
—T. C. J.

To my mom, Daisy
—F. A.

Contents

1
What Dom Found
in the Book

Dom was at the Mundytown library when it opened. She wore a bandanna around her head, squishing her pigtails. And a leather eye patch with a shiny gold *P* for "pirate" covered her eye. Her brother, Rafi, had given her the patch before she left home. Along with a compass.

"Nice look, Dominguita!" Mrs. Booker, the librarian, looked up over reading glasses. "What can I do for you?"

"Captain Dom," she corrected. "You know Dominguita means 'little Sunday' in Spanish, right? No one will respect a pirate named after a day of the week!"

"Sorry for that, Captain Dom. I can see how that could be a problem." Mrs. Booker straightened some papers on her desk. Then she nodded. "You continuing your pirate studies?"

Dom didn't quite know what to say. She still loved the books Mrs. Booker had given her. The ones about Anne Bonny and Mary Read—the best pirates ever. And she didn't want to hurt the librarian's feelings. "I'm not done with studying. Honest. But I think we're ready to actually do something, you know? Like look for treasure."

"Treasure?"

"Me and my mates. Pancho Sanchez and this new girl who's visiting her grandmother. Her name's Steph. We're going on a pirate adventure."

"I see."

"I need two copies of *Treasure Island.* One for

each of them. You can't be a pirate without reading *Treasure Island*."

"I can't agree with you more." Mrs. Booker touched the mouse in her hand to wake up her computer. "You already checked the shelves?"

Dom nodded. "Couldn't find any. My brother, Rafi, agreed to make us a treasure map, so that we can actually look for something. But we want to really act like pirates."

After a few clicks, the librarian shook her head. "We do own two. . . . Looks like someone checked them both out a couple of days ago."

"Hmm," Dom said. "How about another library? Anything close?"

"Wait, wait. We have our Special Books Collection in the basement. I think we have one there." She reached for a notebook swollen with yellow, curling pages. "The librarian before me couldn't get rid of some books. I loved her for it."

After turning a few pages, Mrs. Booker gave a little happy cry. "Yep. Looks like we're in luck."

If there was anything Dom liked better than a book, it was an old book. She kept twelve adventure books her grandmother had read as a little girl in the bookcase next to her bed. They were ready to fall apart, but she loved every one of them. Even though her abuela had moved to Florida, the books made Dom feel connected to her in some way. Dom read them all the time. There was no way she'd miss a chance to go down to the basement to see other old books.

She followed Mrs. Booker down the twisty steps without being invited. The smell in the stacks made her as happy as the smell of sweet buñuelos.

And it made her sneeze.

Which startled Mrs. Booker.

And made her look back.

Caught!

"Sorry, sorry, sorry," Dom said. "I know I shouldn't have come...."

"Are you kidding?" Mrs. Booker said. "You're welcome here! I love this place too!"

The librarian stopped at a table that stretched from side to side at the end of the room. The label above it said SPECIAL BOOKS COLLECTION. Books were piled four deep in neat columns. The first book Dom saw was *Little Women.*

"Mmmm." Mrs. Booker's fingers ran over the columns. "*K, M, R.* It should be here." She stopped at the fourth column over, bottom row, and lifted books until she found the one she was looking for. She blew the dust off the cover and handed it to Dom. "See, I told you it was beautiful—all yours."

This was a good time to start using pirate talk, Dom thought.

"It'll be pure gold to me, I promise."

✕ ✕ ✕

With a wave, Dom left the librarian. Pancho and Steph were waiting for her at Yuca, Yuca, the restaurant that belonged to Pancho's uncle. El Señor Prieto had agreed to feed them during their recent knightly adventures if Dom swept his sidewalk.

She should run. Her mates were waiting, ready to set out on the treasure hunt.

But something about the old book called to her.

She wanted to touch it. Smell its oldness. Take it all in.

By herself.

She stopped at a table by the door and traced the gold letters on the red cover with her fingers. They were barely raised, rounded. She opened it. Carefully. As if it were holy. It was printed in 1947. A couple of years before her abuela was born.

It was not like any other book she'd read. It was crackly, yellow. Some of the type was fancy. Very fancy. With full-color pictures of fighting pirates and black-and-white sketches scattered in the chapters.

Dom thumbed through the loose, worn pages. And there, between pages 168 and 169, she found a flyer. Folded. Pink.

An advertisement for Kowalski's Grocery!

Dom smiled. Mr. Kowalski had helped in their knightly adventure too. He'd made her a knight!

Next to Kowalski's ad was one for Beauty Is You! on Grant Street. That beauty shop was Smart Clips now. That's where Dom's mami got her hair cut. The bottom half of the flyer said the carnival would be in Mundytown from June 20 to June 23. What year? It didn't say. Not on that side. She flipped it over.

And stopped breathing.

On the other side was a map.

X marked a spot.

2

What Dom Did at Yuca, Yuca

Dom barreled into Yuca, Yuca. Her breathing exploded in short, loud bursts. "I. Found. A. M-m-map. Ifoundamap. Ifoundamap."

"Whoa! Whoa! What about 'Shiver my timbers' and 'Ahoy, mates'?" Pancho was tall and hefty. He wore a twisted bandanna to hold the mass of black hair on his head away from his forehead. A plastic sword hung from his belt.

"You mean Rafi already gave you the map?"

Steph scrunched her forehead. Her freckles danced. She was not dressed like a pirate.

"No. No! Well, yes. We have a map." Dom drew her crew into a huddle. "But not from Rafi. I have something better. Just now. At the library. I found a treasure map. A real treasure map!"

"But why don't we wait and use Rafi's map?" Steph said.

"This treasure map is *real*. I promise!" Dom whispered, holding up the book. "I found it between pages 168 and 169."

Dom didn't wait for her mates to answer. "It's like the map in *Treasure Island*. It has notes and two Xs and the numbers ten and thirty-seven."

Now Pancho and Steph nodded. Maybe they were getting it.

"I can't wait to pretend to find the treasure with it," Steph said.

"THIS IS NOT PRETEND!" Dom yelled. "THIS IS A REAL TREASURE MAP!"

Everyone in the restaurant looked up. Her mates. El Señor Prieto. The cooks and waiters. Even a blond girl who was having flan at ten o'clock in the morning.

Dom straightened up. "It's a real *pretend* treasure map, Steph. Rafi made it for us. You're right." Her voice was the most normal she could manage. And loud. So everyone could hear her. "And WE NEED TO WEIGH ANCHOR AND SEARCH FOR IT. RIGHT NOW." She pulled her two friends out of their chairs and through the door of the restaurant. She ran. She didn't stop until she was three blocks away. She knew she should have waited for Steph, but it was as if she were being pushed by a hurricane. Finally, she stopped in an alley between apartment buildings, where she plopped down on the steps by a back door of a building.

× × ×

"What was that all about?" Pancho asked, panting, after he and Steph caught up to her.

"I can't believe I blabbed! I told everybody about the map."

"But isn't it a pretend treasure map?" Steph dropped next to Dom.

"It's not!" Dom cried. "It's real. Real. Real. I know it is. And now everybody knows we have a *real* treasure map."

Pancho waved her off. "Don't worry. Nobody pays attention to us. They don't care."

"But I talked so loud!"

Pancho shrugged. "Last week we were knights. This week we're pirates. My uncle knows we're playing. Everyone knows we're playing."

Dom sighed. "You think?"

"Sure. Nobody takes us seriously."

"Oh." Dom wasn't sure which was worse, giving away the secret or that no one took them seriously.

Steph patted her on the back. "Come on, Cap'n," she said. "Show us the map!"

Dom pulled it out. She held the precious paper by the corners. Her fingers shook as she smoothed it out on her lap. Even with the noises of the street, their breathing was all she could hear.

Steph whistled. "Could be for real."

"It's real," Pancho agreed.

Dom grinned. "I told you!"

She traced the shape on the paper with her index finger. A rectangle. Sort of. One of the two long sides was missing a half circle. As if someone had taken out a chunk with a cookie cutter. There was a small x. There was also a larger X, in blue. It was north of the small x.

Which was only north if you agreed that the random, half-finished arrow on the right of the paper pointed north.

Which may not be a good thing to agree to.

Because it looked more like a chicken's foot.

And there was absolutely nothing else that showed north.

Whoever drew the map scattered four lines with circles on top—like lollipops—inside the rectangle. The number thirty-seven was an addition. In different ink.

But then, at the bottom of the page, scraggly, like the X, a note: *The sun will show when it's highest in the sky. Dial, diagonal, park.*

In neat handwriting: *Ten feet from X to x.*

All three stared at the paper for more than a minute. Dom broke the silence. "Wow, huh? It's good enough to yell *huzzah!*"

Pancho nodded. "Shiver my timbers, it's a puzzle."

Steph shook her head. "But it doesn't say where this is. It could be on another planet."

Steph was right. The buccaneers in *Treasure Island* knew where the treasure was. They had coordinates. They knew hills, and creeks, and coves. They could use a compass to find the place. But Dom still had a feeling this was a *real* map.

"So here's the deal," Dom said. "The flyer is about Mundytown. The book was in the Mundytown library. We look in Mundytown. My mami won't let me go anywhere else anyway."

Steph shook her head. "I just don't want to be going all over everywhere. That's why Rafi's map . . ."

Dom had to get Steph to agree, to get off this kick about Rafi's map. "I think gold dust of you," she told her friend. "I want you to be ship's doctor. That's the next most important post after captain."

Steph scrunched her face again. But it was a happier face.

"Whoa! I'm glad we're out of *that* clove hitch," Dom said.

"Knotty problem," Pancho translated before Steph even asked.

"Now we're getting somewhere, buccaneers!" Dom gave them each a high five. "Pancho, will you be first mate?"

Pancho saluted. "Aye, aye, Cap'n."

"So what do we need?"

"It talks about parks, right?" Pancho pointed to the map. "We need maps to figure out where parks are. And a compass."

"Gran gave me lots of maps so I won't get lost now that I'm living here."

"Rafi gave me a compass before I left this morning."

"How about swords and gullies?" Pancho asked.

"Gullies?" Steph asked.

"Knives," Pancho said. "Pirate knives. Pirates always have swords and gullies. Who knows? If we get hot on the trail of this treasure and someone finds out . . ." Pancho patted the plastic sword hanging from his belt.

"I'll see what I can find at Fuentes Salvage," Dom said. "But we might as well forget the gullies. I don't think he'll let us have any even if he has some."

"Shovels, pics, and stuff to dig treasure with," said Steph.

"Well, jump on the yardarm, Doc, that's a brilliant idea!"

"Lunch!" Pancho said. "I'll run back to Yuca, Yuca and get ham biscuits."

It was time to wrap things up, the captain thought. "Eight bells. Forenoon watch. Bring your stuff to the conference room at the library. I don't think we should meet at Yuca, Yuca for now."

"Aye, aye, Cap'n!" Pancho saluted, and turned to leave.

Steph followed him. "Wait, wait. What's eight bells, anyway?"

"It's ship's time," Pancho said. "Noon."

"I'm gonna have to read *Treasure Island* tonight."

"Watch the movie," Pancho said. "It'll be faster."

3
What Dom Found at Fuentes Salvage

El Señor Fuentes had provided some of the equipment for Dom's knightly adventure. His junk shop was full of useless things waiting to become useful. Dom was sure it was the best place in Mundytown to find pirate stuff.

"Hey, Señor Fuentes," Dom called.

"Good morning, good knight," Señor Fuentes answered from the back room of the junk shop.

"How's your quest going?"

"I'm done being a knight, remember? I brought back my armor and my helmet."

"Ah yes, I remember." Señor Fuentes stepped into the main room. "What are you today?"

Dom touched her bandanna. "I'm a pirate now. Captain Dom. In search of treasure."

"Treasure?"

How much should she tell el Señor Fuentes? Sure, she could trust him. But maybe not yet. Maybe she'd tell him the truth later. "Yeah. You know. Rafi's making us pretend maps. We're playing."

"Well, then. You'll be wanting a shovel, I bet." Señor Fuentes slipped away from the counter.

"One would be helpful, and two even better. And picks."

"Hmm. One shovel I have. But picks . . ." El Señor Fuentes raised the eyebrow over his blue eye in thought. The eyebrow over the brown eye stayed still. It didn't seem to be working on the problem. "No picks right now," he finally said. "Sorry."

Dom nodded. At least he had a shovel.

"What else?"

"We need something to protect ourselves, you know, if we meet any other desperate pirates."

"Mmmm." Both of the eyebrows were working on that question. "We can figure something out."

They looked some more.

El Señor Fuentes picked up a metal thing with a wooden handle. It ended up in a shallow V. "This dandelion weeder might be useful. You can stick it in your belt." El Señor Fuentes demonstrated.

Dom wasn't wearing a belt.

El Señor Fuentes handed her a metal hook. "Here, take this. It's a carabiner. You can hang it from your belt loop and stick the weeder in that."

Dom did as he said. The dandelion tool was a bit rusty, and very dull. But an enemy might think it was a sword from far enough away. It worked. "Jump on the yardarm, it's brilliant! Just brilliant!"

El Señor Fuentes's blue eye winked. "Without a doubt, Captain. Without a doubt."

Dom looked around some more. "How about a sea chest? Billy Bones in *Treasure Island* had a sea chest. It would be awesome to have one."

"Hmmm. Hard to carry around. How about a canvas bag? Sailors carry canvas bags. Plenty of room for doubloons and such. You can sling it over your shoulder."

"Shiver my timbers, mate. Do you have three? That way we could split the weight."

El Señor Fuentes pulled down three bags. "Now, what else?"

"A spyglass would be nice. An easy-to-carry one."

"No spyglass. But I have some binoculars. . . ." He handed Dom a dusty pair.

Which promptly broke in the middle.

Sending one of the lenses clattering to the floor in pieces.

Dom picked up the other lens. She could hold it with one hand!

"Well?"

"Perfect. Almost as good as a spyglass." Dom thought a little more. "You wouldn't know where I could get a parrot, do you?" Long John Silver's parrot in *Treasure Island* said "Pieces of Eight" and all sorts of bad words.

Señor Fuentes laughed. "Afraid not, Captain Dom. But I'll keep my eyes and ears open for one. I imagine you'd like a trained one? One that can speak?"

"That would be pure gold, mate," she said. "Pure gold."

Dom couldn't think of anything else she needed. She bundled the tools into the sailor bags. "Just like last time? I'm borrowing this?"

"Absolutely. You bring the stuff back in pretty good shape and there won't be any charge. No charge at all."

Dom headed for the door, but el Señor Fuentes called her back.

"Captain Dom, uh, please give your abuela my regards next time you talk to her."

"Of course!" Dom said. And of course she would. Actually, Abuela needed to know about this right now. She punched in her grandmother's number on her way back to the library.

"Ay, Dominguita, mi amor. It's so nice to talk to you. It's been so long," Abuela said.

It hadn't been. She'd texted Abuela last Sunday and talked to her on Monday, Tuesday, and Wednesday. That's why Abuela wasn't living with Dom's family anymore. Because she forgot. Now she was living in Florida with her sister, who could keep an eye on her all the time.

22

"I'm a pirate now, remember, Abuela? Like *Treasure Island!*"

"Oh. A pirate. How nice."

Dom looked all the way around. She wanted to make sure no one would hear her. She knew how to get Abuela's attention. "We found a real map. *A real treasure map.* We'll have to figure out what the map is to, but I know it's a treasure. A TREASURE!"

"A treasure!" All of a sudden Abuela's voice was excited. "You'll be Jim Hawkins like you were Don Quijote?"

At least Abuela still knew Jim Hawkins was the main character in *Treasure Island.* "Actually, I'm the captain. I like being the captain. Captain Dom."

"Well, then, Captain Dom. May you have fair winds! Send me messages in a bottle when you get a chance."

"YESSSS!" That was the real Abuela. "And el Señor Fuentes said to say 'Hi.'"

Dom ran the rest of the way to the library.

4
What They Know and What They Don't Know

After asking Mrs. Booker if they could use the conference room, Dom dropped the sailor bags against the wall. Then she made a sign saying OFFICERS' CABIN. She taped it to the door.

When she finished, she pulled out a piece of paper and began dividing it into columns. It was a trick she'd learned for solving problems.

"Here I am, eight bells sharp." Pancho dropped

tracing paper on the table and plopped down next to Dom.

"Ta-da!" Steph was wearing a bandanna around her neck. She'd drawn an anchor in marker on her forearm. After dropping a cookie tin and a map of Mundytown on the table, she added a shovel to the stuff by the wall.

"And I brought food!" Pancho pulled out the ham sandwiches his uncle had sent from Yuca, Yuca. He handed each person two ham biscuits. "Mrs. Booker says don't leave any crumbs on the table," he added.

For a couple of minutes the sound of chomping was all you could hear in the room. Then Pancho pushed his chair back.

"So where's that treasure map? I'll start making copies."

"Copies?" Dom raised her eyebrows.

"Yeah! I'll trace it without the words or the Xs. In case we need to show it to someone like Long John Silver."

"Shiver my timbers, mate. . . ." Dom nodded, surprised.

"Yo, ho, ho and a bottle of pop, Cap'n!" Pancho leaned toward Dom to make his point. "You're not the only one who read *Treasure Island.*"

Dom gave her mate and her doc high fives. She should have known. Pancho was already very good at talking Pirate.

"I guess the doc needs a map too, right?" Steph asked.

Dom decided to begin the discussion while the mate and the doc copied their maps. "So, what do we need to know?"

"What's the treasure?" Steph said.

Dom wrote it in the WHAT WE NEED TO FIGURE OUT column.

"Could be some family's silver, their jewelry." Dom scribbled that.

Pancho shook his head, but Dom didn't pay attention. No idea was a bad idea.

"Some kind of letter with a secret," Steph said.

Dom wrote it down.

"How 'bout loot from a robbery?" Pancho said.

Dom scribbled again.

The three crew members stared at the piece of paper.

"It doesn't make sense to bury jewelry or a letter, right? And have a map?" Steph said.

"She's right. You'd use a safe for that," Pancho said. "My bet is we're looking for *stolen* jewels. Or money."

"Wait, wait," Dom said. "We can't just forget the other ideas, right?"

"We can if they don't make sense," Pancho said. "Look, we can't figure out anything about family jewels or letters. But we *could* find a robbery in the newspaper, right?"

"That makes sense," Steph said.

"Okay," Dom said. "We'll look at a robbery . . . first."

All three crew members shifted in their seats. Steph took the lead. "It happened in Mundytown," she said.

Dom nodded. She wrote it down in the column labeled WHAT WE KNOW.

"We know there are four trees," the mate said.

"Trees?"

"They're not lollipops."

Dom looked at Steph. She nodded. Dom put it in the WHAT WE KNOW column. In the WHAT WE NEED TO FIND OUT column, she wrote, WHERE CAN WE FIND FOUR TREES INSIDE A RECTANGLE WITH A HALF-CIRCLE CHUNK MISSING? Their neighborhood was full of apartment buildings. Not many trees.

"What does the number mean? The thirty-seven?" Dom was writing as she talked.

"Distance between trees?"

"Yeah. But remember, there's that word 'dial,'" Pancho said. "Do we need to use the number ten, too? Ten-three-seven?"

"Nah," Doc said. "It's thirty-seven. Numbers are close together. And ten's part of something else."

"What about dial? Huh? How does that make sense?"

The doc shrugged.

Dom scribbled furiously: *Numbers = Dial? Combination? Distance? Could be feet. Could be steps.*

Adult steps? Where are trees that are 37 feet apart or 37 steps apart in Mundytown? DIAGONAL? Is the 10 only between X and little x?

"And why is there a big X and a little x?" Steph tapped her finger on the paper to let Dom know she should write that down too.

"Could be one is where the key is and the other where the treasure is."

"In *Treasure Island* there was treasure at both."

"What we really need to know is when," Dom said. "When did the robbery happen? Or when was the loot buried?"

Mate Pancho lifted his head from his tracing. "We know it was buried in June."

Both Dom and Steph started. "How do we know that?"

"'The sun will show when it's highest in the sky . . . ,'" Pancho said, quoting the map. "The summer solstice. When the sun's highest in the sky."

"Split my sides!" Captain Dom said. "Pure gold."

"So it happened between June 20 and June 22, depending on the year," Steph said.

Dom nodded. "What if it's just talking about noon? When the sun is highest in the sky each day?"

"The carnival was in town from June twentieth through the twenty-third. I think it's the solstice, but it works either way. Write it down."

The captain did.

"Buried between June twentieth and twenty-second. Could have been stolen anytime," Pancho corrected. "Right?"

Both the doc and the captain agreed. "But it would have been stolen right around that same time."

Everyone agreed with that, too.

"I say it couldn't have happened before the book came to the library."

"I bet Mrs. Booker knows when it was bought."

"So when we check the newspapers . . . ," Pancho said.

"Wait, wait!" Steph said. "We can get a really good date. No one checked that book out after the map went in it, right? Anyone checks it out finds the map. And if *they* find the map, *we* don't find the map. Start there and work backward."

"Well, split my sides, Doc," Pancho said. "Now you're making sense."

Dom scrambled over to the table where she'd left the old book, and her crew followed. She opened the back flap. There, stamped on a lined piece of paper glued to the last page, was the date. The last time the book was checked out: June 25, 1967.

"Wait, wait," Pancho said. "Wouldn't the librarians find the map when they put the book in the stacks?"

"THEY DIDN'T!" both Steph and Dom yelled.

Pencils dropped, and chairs toppled. In seconds Pancho, Dom, and Steph surrounded Mrs. Booker's desk.

"We need to see newspapers from around June 25, 1967."

5

What They Found in the Newspapers

"**W**hat are you looking for?" Mrs. Booker asked.

The three friends glanced at one another. What could they say?

Dom figured they might as well be honest. Sort of. "We're trying to find robberies."

"But we don't *know* of any robberies. We're just checking," Steph said. "You know. Hoping for something, and then we can start our treasure hunt."

"Like we did the knightly quest," Pancho added. "We'll have more fun if we have some real stuff to go on."

"I get it," Mrs. Booker said. "Something you could use for your treasure."

All three nodded as if they were bobbleheads.

Mrs. Booker started walking toward a file cabinet. "Just around that date?"

"For now," Dom said. "You wouldn't know of any, would you?"

"Robberies? Back then? I wasn't even born!" She pulled two small cardboard boxes tied with string from a file cabinet. "Here's where we can find out."

× × ×

Mrs. Booker pointed to two machines by the far wall of the officers' cabin. "These are microfiche machines," she said. "The way they kept copies of newspapers back then. Like scans. Copies of the newspapers are in these little film boxes. Scroll through to find what you want. Dates are at the top. Check the Metro section. That's where the police reports are."

Pancho parked himself in front of one machine. The librarian took a reel of film from the first box. She threaded it over some rollers and between glass plates. It was the *Morning Gazette*. Steph took the other machine with the *Evening Tribune*.

"Those are big town newspapers," Mrs. Booker told the crew. "They may not cover Mundytown crimes. The *Mundytown Weekly*'s in the basement. Far-right corner."

Dom didn't wait for Mrs. Booker. She shot down the basement stairs. The boxes were exactly where the librarian had said.

She hauled the box labeled MUNDYTOWN WEEKLY—1967 upstairs and plopped it in the middle of the table. While Pancho and Steph complained they weren't finding anything and the machines made them cross-eyed, she dove in. She thumbed through the issues until she found the Thursday, June 22, copy.

Nothing.

No surprise. Maybe the heist didn't make that week's deadline. She could barely hold her hands still. The next issue would have it for sure.

But there was no issue dated June 29. She quickly searched all copies in the box—none out of place. She counted to confirm it—only fifty-one.

The newspaper they wanted was missing.

She told the crew. "That's strange, right?"

The mate and the doc stopped searching on the microfiche machines.

"There have to be some other clues," Pancho said. "In the *Weekly*. The next couple of weeks the police were looking for the robber, right? And it might have happened weeks before the twenty-second. There has to be something!"

Each of them took weeklies dated around the missing paper. They searched every page.

Nothing. Until . . .

Two faces looked up at Dom. Familiar, but not really. As if she knew the boys in the school pictures in the paper but couldn't remember their names. She read the caption. "'Emilio Fuentes and Jake Kowalski Will Report for Duty on June 26.'" They had joined the Marines. They would be off to Vietnam.

"Look at this!" She pointed to the names.

"*Your* Mr. Fuentes?" Pancho asked.

"Fuentes Salvage?" That was Steph.

Dom nodded. "I can't tell if it's Mr. Kowalski. He's got a woolly mustache now. But look—look at Emilio

Fuentes's eyes. One is lighter than the other. It's him. I promise."

"He'll know what happened that year. He'll know about a robbery!"

Chairs toppled again. Dom's heart pounded like waves during a storm.

They cleaned up the room and handed the microfiche reels and *Mundytown Weekly* copies to Mrs. Booker and thanked her. They were close to knowing if there was a real treasure.

6
What El Señor Fuentes Remembered

El Señor Fuentes remembered a robbery! It happened right after he graduated from high school in 1967.

"Jake Kowalski got all beat up," he said. "They knocked him out when they robbed the store."

"W-w-w-wait." Dom couldn't believe it. "Jake Kowalski is Mr. Kowalski? From Kowalski's Grocery?"

Pancho leaned on the counter. "Robbed?"

Steph's voice broke. "Wh-when was that?"

"Must have been . . ." El Señor Fuentes scratched the eyebrow above his brown eye. "Let's see. What's the date of that newspaper? Does it say when we graduated?"

Dom handed him a copy of the article. "It says when you left for boot camp—June twenty-sixth."

"That's it. We had a week. Jake Kowalski and me. But the store was robbed a few days after we graduated. Say the twenty-second or the twenty-third. Jake was working. He ended up in the hospital."

"He never went to Vietnam?"

"Oh yeah. We both went. Thankfully, the robbers didn't hurt him that bad." Señor Fuentes shook his head. "They never found that money, though."

Dom's head buzzed. "The treasure's Mr. Kowalski's!"

"Treasure, Dominguita? You've used that word a few times now." El Señor Fuentes looked confused.

"You know . . ." Pancho tried to save Dom. "We're pirates and all now. Like we were knights before. We're looking for treasure. Any kind of treasure."

39

"Ah," Señor Fuentes said.

Steph pulled Dom away. "And we'd better get going."

Dom ran out of the store.

"I did it again!" she muttered when they were a block away. "I blabbed."

"Yeah, but Señor Fuentes doesn't care, Dominguita!"

Dom's eyes shot lightning bolts at Pancho. "*Dom!* And I guess we can start to figure out where that treasure is. We have to find it. We have to find it for Mr. Kowalski."

"Yep," Steph said. "We'd better get going."

They stopped at the monument to Saint Francis in front of the Catholic church. It had a bench and a rock to sit on with statues of small animals all around.

Pancho pulled out his half-eaten ham biscuit. "Let's finish our hardtack while we figure this out."

Steph pulled her sandwich and a Mundytown map out of her sailor bag. "First question: Where in Mundytown can we find four trees?"

"Maybe things changed since 1967."

Dom stopped. Pancho was probably right. But how could they know where trees had been in 1967? Some could have died or been cut down. "We know the park is the only place to find four trees around here," Dom said. "We have to go with what we know now. And the word 'park' *is* on the map."

Steph put her finger on the green areas on the Mundytown map. "There are exactly three parks in Mundytown—Grant, Washington, and the one with the fountain—the one near Gran's house."

"Monroe Park," Dom said.

"There's one on the other side of the bridge." Pancho showed them another green area just over the line between Mundytown and the city. "It could be that."

"Yeah, yeah." Dom subtracted in her head. "It's about forty blocks. The bridge is on Sixty-Seventh. We can go on the bus."

"The bus?" Steph asked quietly.

"Yes, the number fifty-seven bus," Pancho said. "My mom and I go by there on the way to the dentist. I've seen the sign for the park."

"Yeah!" Dom was about to give Pancho a high five when she noticed Steph.

"What's wrong?"

"Nothing. It's just . . . I—I—won't be able to go."

"I have fare for us—don't worry." Dom pulled out her bus card. "I always have three or four extra trips on it in case of emergencies."

Pancho had a card too. "Enough for both ways. For all of us."

Steph shook her head. "No, it's not that. My grandmother won't let me. I've never even ridden a bus."

Dom and Pancho froze. They rode a town bus to school every day.

"She worries. My parents left her in charge of me. She thinks they'll be mad if she lets me go far from her." Steph wasn't the doc anymore. Her voice was about to crack into a million pieces.

"Oh." Pancho's voice wasn't much better.

"I bet I can talk my brother, Rafi, into coming. After he's done working. He's fifteen, almost sixteen," Dom said.

Steph shook her head. "My grandma's scared to death when I'm with you guys. She's only letting me do it because I don't have any friends here."

Pancho looked down at his shoes.

"Here's the deal," Dom finally said, pointing to the map. "Today we'll walk to Grant Park. Only twenty blocks. We don't have to take the bus. We'll check it out. Tomorrow, Washington. Even closer, remember? You walked there when we fought the giant. Then Monroe."

"And if none of them work?" Steph wouldn't let herself get excited.

"We'll go to your house. Tomorrow afternoon. We talk your grandmother into letting you take the bus. She can even come with us if she wants to. One for all and all for one." Dom raised both her hands for high fives.

"Wrong book," Pancho said, but he gave her a high five anyway.

✗ ✗ ✗

Grant Park was like paradise. The entrance led through an archway of trees to a huge playground. Slides started high in the sky before spilling in four different directions. Some even twisted like insane pretzels. One shot down through a tunnel. You could grab monkey bars to go over a sand pit. The swings could fly to the stratosphere if you had the guts.

"Look at the basketball courts!"

"And soccer fields!"

"Where has this place been all my life?" Pancho turned with his mouth open.

"You've never been here?" Steph asked.

"Our bus comes a couple of blocks away. I've seen the sign, but I've never stopped," Dom said.

"Me neither," Pancho said. "But I am from now on. This is awesome."

"There's anything you could want." Steph spread her arms wide.

"Except four trees."

Pancho was right. Trees surrounded the park. Forests. With paths cutting through them. But four trees? Inside a rectangle? Not here.

"Might as well play before we walk home again," Pancho said.

Dom stomped her foot. "No way! We have to rule out this place for sure."

"And why?"

"That's what Sherlock Holmes would do."

Pancho bit his lip. "I thought we were pirates, not detectives. You're mixing up your books again."

"We're looking for Mr. Kowalski's money. Sherlock Holmes might help. Anyway, we need to figure out if this is definitely not it."

"But it's not!" Pancho pushed an empty swing. "I don't see anywhere you find four trees in a rectangle with a hole cut out of one side. Do you?"

"Look at all those trees around us! We won't know unless we look for them inside the forest. Let's walk around the paths."

"Aw geez, forget the paths inside the forest. Let's play!" Pancho whined.

Dom stood strong. "What if we miss it and miss Kowalski's treasure?"

"I'm not trying to get out of walking," Steph said,

"but those numbers mean something. They mean feet. Or steps. I saw a map of the paths when we came in. Maybe we can figure it out without spending time walking."

Steph slid her finger over the map when they got to it. "No clearings in these woods."

"Nope."

"Oh well." Dom's flat tone left no room for hope. "It's not this park. But I'm glad we checked it out. It's the right way to do an investigation."

"And now we can play!" Pancho punched the air.

"Uhh . . ." Steph didn't join in the air punching.

"We'll ride the bus home," Pancho said. "We'll get back in plenty of time. You don't have to tell your grandmother. Besides, you're with us. She loves us, right?"

7

What Steph Brought with Her the Next Morning

"Cool!" Rafi said when Dom got home that night. "Latest in pirate wear?"

"Fuentes Salvage," Dom said.

She talked the day over with her brother. She showed him the map.

"It's for real," Rafi confirmed. "And you figured out it's the robbery of Kowalski's Grocery?"

Dom nodded. "I know for sure."

"Woo-hee! Abuela will love this!" Rafi punched

his fist in the air. He and Dom had decided, during her knightly adventures, that Rafi would write books for Abuela to remember Dom's deeds. "*And* the *Mundytown Weekly* will love it! If you keep having adventures, the paper might even give me a job."

Dom had to get back to the mystery. "So what do you think? You think they're trees?"

"Yup. That's a sign people use for trees." Rafi leaned back. "But it beats me where you'd find four trees in Mundytown laid out like that."

"I don't get the dial thing, either," Dom said. "Why would it say 'dial'?"

"Sundial?"

"Mmm. Hadn't thought about that. And the numbers? Ten and thirty-seven."

"Ten you can tell. That's the distance between big X and little x. Thirty-seven could be the distance between trees."

"But there's four trees and one number. . . . Unless . . ." Dom fiddled with the handle of her "sword" as she thought. Then she reached into her sailor bag and pulled out a piece of tracing paper.

She put it over the map and put a circle at the base of each "tree."

"You're smart as paint, Cap'n," Rafi said. "It's a square!"

"Yup. It's not perfect, but I bet you it's a thirty-seven-foot or thirty-seven-step square."

Rafi drew two lines across the square and put his finger where they crossed. "And *that* is where x marks the spot."

Dom lifted his finger. Below it, through the tracing paper, she could see the little x. "Diagonal. That's one of the words. Where the two diagonals meet is the little x!"

"Fair winds will be with you tomorrow for sure. Tell me your deeds and I'll write about them."

"I'll tell you my deeds when I've done them," Dom said, and she went to set the table.

✕ ✕ ✕

Pancho was on a computer in the officers' cabin the next morning when Dom got there.

"Charting our course, Cap'n," he said. "And our course won't take us to the park across the river."

"Why not?" Dom snapped. Her mother had made her late that morning. She wanted Dom's help with folding the wash. Then she'd swept the front of Yuca, Yuca for their lunch. She didn't want a problem now. Especially not with their treasure hunt. "We have to look at everything!"

"There's nothing there!" the mate said, turning the screen toward her. "Look!"

He had pulled up a street view of the park. And zoomed. There were tennis courts, and running tracks. There was a pool. And an outdoor fitness track. But trees? Not one. Not even surrounding it. The park was bordered in chain-link fence.

Dom could kick herself. After what happened the day before, she should have checked that out herself. "At least Doc won't have to ask her grandmother."

Dom dropped the lunch bag el Señor Prieto had sent for them on the table. She was about to tell her mate what she and Rafi had figured out when the door opened.

"Ahoy, mates. I hear you're looking for treasure."
A tall boy with Steph broke into a huge grin as he
stepped into the officers' cabin. He looked to be thirteen or fourteen.

Steph looked like she wanted the earth to swallow her whole. "He caught up to me at the door to
the library. Said my grandmother sent him."

"My name is J.L." The boy's blond hair drooped
over his blue eyes. He was wearing a T-shirt with
a very detailed tarantula on the front. He dropped

into a chair. "Steph's grandmother was worried last night, at my aunt's beauty shop. Auntie Em called her this morning, after Steph left. She volunteered me to babysit. The grandmother thinks it's better if someone older is with you. If I'm with you, Steph can do whatever you guys do." He puffed out his chest, like a walrus.

"Aw, come on!" Pancho said.

Steph's ears burned.

Dom was about to explode. Now they were in another clove hitch. She wanted to find Mr. Kowalski's money. *And* give it back to him. What if this pushy guy got in the way? She looked at Steph's miserable face and said the only thing she could say. "AARGH!"

Pancho looked at Dom and then he looked back at Steph. "We're not going anywhere far now," he said. "Maybe we should call your grandmother and tell her that."

Steph shook her head, miserable.

"Let's call her! We don't need him." Now it was Pancho who was turning red.

"I can't call her," Steph said. "She's . . . she's . . . Well, she has her rules. And if she sent this guy, then I can't call her. I won't call her."

Silence blanketed the room.

"Honest!" J.L. said. "I love *Treasure Island*. I'll just follow you guys around, or take you where you want to go. I'll stay out of the way. I promise."

"Look," Steph said. "I'll go home. It's more important that you guys keep up the investigation."

"No, no, no," J.L. said. Then he spoke directly to Dom. "You look like you're in charge here. Tell me your plans. Show me your maps. I can help find the treasure."

Dom beamed. She liked what the boy said. Maybe they should let him into the investigation. More important, she knew how bad Steph felt. The captain had to take care of her crew.

Pancho scowled. "We need a council." He dragged Dom and Steph out of the officers' cabin. "I don't like this guy."

"Chill. It's clear sailing, mate. If Steph's grandma

wants him to go with us, what's wrong with that?" Dom asked.

For a long second, Pancho didn't say anything. Steph wouldn't even look up.

Finally, Pancho turned to Steph. "Did you tell your grandmother the map is real?"

Steph nodded. The color of her face almost blended with her hair. "He knows so much. The only way he'd know is if she told him. So that means she really did send him. I told you. You guys don't know about me and my grandmother. She's taking care of me while my parents are off . . . working. . . . I can't make things hard on her."

Pancho punched a shelf outside the meeting room. "I hate that he's saying all this pirate stuff. Like he read *Treasure Island* or something."

Dom shrugged. "What's wrong with that? He loves the book! He said so."

"I'll tell you what's wrong with that," Pancho whispered so loud, Dom was sure J.L. heard it inside the room. "I had to reread the book to remember my pirate words. He wouldn't know all those words if he

55

didn't just read the book. And *somebody* just checked out two copies of *Treasure Island* at the library. And *somebody* took that *Mundytown Weekly*. The one that's missing. I saw the checkout sheet on the box. It was checked out two days ago. It's just too weird this dude shows up at just the right time. He's looking for the same thing we are. I know he is."

Dom wished she could tell Pancho that he was wrong, but she had noticed the same thing.

Still.

She was the captain, and she couldn't have Steph feeling bad.

She had to decide.

She nodded. Hard. As if trying to tell herself that what she was about to do was the right thing. "We all go, or nobody goes. I know it's the wrong book, but it's all for one and one for all. And since Steph goes, that kid goes."

"Hrmph." Pancho turned away.

"We won't tell him anything," Dom called after him.

Before Pancho had a chance to talk back, J.L. opened the door to the officers' cabin.

"Hey," he told Dom, looking into her eyes. "I get it. You don't want to tell me anything about your game. I don't blame you. But if my aunt finds out I didn't do what she said, I'm gonna be in real trouble. My aunt loves Steph's grandmother. She wants to do something nice for her. You don't want to get in the way of that, do you?"

Dom had already decided, but even if she wanted to, now it would be really hard to turn him down.

She took a deep breath. "We're all going," she said. "And that's the way it is. He might be able to help us."

Pancho still stared at her. Steph looked halfway between grateful and surprised.

They could think whatever they wanted. She was the captain. They were already late.

"Mate," she said to Pancho. "Chart us a course for Twenty-Seventh and Washington. We'll put in at the Holland House to see Ms. Belle first. Maybe we'll even see Roco."

She was sure that mentioning Ms. Belle, the Holland House, and Roco would make her crew happier.

Ms. Belle owned the restaurant with the windmill they'd fought during their knightly adventure. She had promised them free lemonade for life when they rescued a little boy and Rafi wrote an article about their adventure. The Holland House had ended up in the newspaper.

Roco was the stray dog who'd played their steed while they were knights. He'd loved Dom, Pancho, and Steph, but Ms. Belle had a never-ending supply of food scraps. The long squatty dog now made his home around the Holland House.

"Hrmph," Pancho said, but he was smiling.

"I guess it's the best thing by a sea mile," Steph said. She had obviously watched the movie the night before.

"Weigh anchor!" Dom headed out of the library.

8

What Juan Largo Said

"Why don't you show me the map?" J.L. asked Dom on the way. "You know four heads are better than three."

Pancho stopped. He squared up to the blond boy. Dom could imagine smoke coming out of his ears. He was not about to let her forget the guy could be a villain.

"You know what, J.L.? We'll be calling you Juan Largo from now on," Pancho declared. Juan Largo meant Long John. Like Long John Silver from *Treasure Island.* Pancho hoped the villain knew Spanish, and he knew that at least Pancho was onto him.

Before Dom could respond, Steph approved the name. "Juan Largo, yes. Great idea. And since you're Juan Largo, here you go." She handed him a piece of paper.

"Juan Largo," the boy said. His smile was big as a whale's as he rushed to unfold the paper. "I love that name." He sauntered on with Dom and tried to look cool while he scanned the map at the same time.

The coolness didn't last long. His forehead scrunched under his blond bangs once he actually saw what was on the paper. Steph had given him the pretend map she'd copied. It didn't have any of the Xs, or numbers, or words. He crushed the paper in his fist. "Is this all?"

"Why?" Steph said. "Were you looking for more, Juan?"

"Yes, Juan?" The new name came easy to Dom too. She had fallen in with her crew as far as the name, especially when the boy was acting like a villain.

Because Dom had also noticed the change. Did Juan Largo know something about the map already? Why had he asked that question?

"I guess you guys still don't trust me," the blond boy said. "You can't tell anything from this map. If you're looking for a treasure, you need to know more. And I guess you're just not telling me." He started walking again.

Dom felt better. It was true. The pretend map didn't even fool Long John Silver in *Treasure Island*. Maybe she was too quick to find fault. Maybe Juan didn't already know anything.

✕ ✕ ✕

The park on Twenty-Seventh and Washington was about three blocks square. They walked and walked along snaking brick paths. Around beds full of rainbow-colored flowers and large patches of thick grass. They walked through a playground.

But it was easy to see this was not the place. There were scattered trees, all right. Scattered everywhere. But they were all way more than thirty-seven feet apart.

Nothing that looked like the four trees in the treasure map.

There was no square like she and Rafi had figured out. Not inside a rectangle.

Some of the flower beds were circles—but not half circles.

Dom was sure this was not the right park, and she could tell the other two agreed. Their shoulders slumped as they got to the farthest end of the park. Strike two!

Actually, strike three. Dom knew the park where they'd met Steph—Monroe Park—it didn't have any trees either. Did they need to change their tack? Did they need to look for something other than trees? Maybe it would be a good idea to actually let Juan Largo help.

But she knew her crew wouldn't like that.

She took a heading toward the Holland House Restaurant at the other corner of the park.

As if her thoughts had brought him, Juan stepped in, next to her. It was as if he wanted to separate her from her mates.

"So. Did you see anything?" Juan Largo asked.

"Look," Dom whispered as she walked next to the tall boy. "I want you to help us. But I have to convince the crew. If I tell you anything now, they'll give me the black spot."

"The black spot?"

Maybe he hadn't read *Treasure Island* after all. "It's a piece of paper with a black smudge on it. If your pirate crew gives you the black spot, it means they're gonna kick you out. You won't be captain anymore." Dom was very serious.

Juan Largo snickered, but then he caught himself. "Oh yeah, I remember. We wouldn't want that to happen."

"I'll talk to them later. I'm sure I can show you the real map in the morning, and together we can all figure it out."

"But I could help you now, if you give me the information now." Juan bent down and got close to Dom's ear. "You know what you're doing. Tell me more. I know there's more on that map."

There it was again. Why was Juan Largo saying that he knew there was more on the map? How could he? Maybe Steph told her grandmother about the numbers and the notes, too.

"I told you—I can't."

"Well, of course. And you're the smartest one of the group. I can tell that. But it's important to find the money, right? Mr. Kowalski's? I just want to help."

"I can't do anything," Dom said. Juan Largo was beginning to soften her up. "The others have to agree."

"No they don't. You're the captain. You have to do what's good for the mission."

Dom shook her head. She was happy that the Holland House Restaurant was only steps away.

✕ ✕ ✕

"The knight gig is done?" Ms. Belle asked when the crew settled at the outside tables. "You're pirates now, I see."

"Yes, ma'am, in search for treasure," Dom said.

Pancho shook his head. Dom could tell he wanted her to shut up.

"And you have a new member?"

"No!" Steph and Pancho both answered without giving Dom a chance.

"I guess—I guess I'm Juan Largo. They gave me a new name even though they haven't decided yet if they'll let me join the group," Juan Largo said in his most charming voice. "I'm babysitting Steph, here. Her grandmother is worried about her."

"Umph!" It was clear that Ms. Belle thought the three of them didn't need babysitting.

"I'll bring you lemonade," Ms. Belle said, heading inside. "And if you want to see your steed, he's by the kitchen door."

Once she left, Juan Largo looked straight at Dom and raised an eyebrow. "You guys probably want to talk," he said. "I'll get some ice cream inside."

"Wait!" Pancho pulled some change from his pocket. "Why don't you bring the rest of us some ice cream while you're there?"

They watched Juan step into the restaurant.

"That'll keep him away for a while," Pancho said.

Dom wanted to see Roco, but it was more important to get her crew to let Juan Largo into the group. "I think we ought to let him help us," she said. "We're in a clove hitch. And four heads *are* better than three."

"Aw, Cap'n!" Pancho slapped the table. "Are you kidding? How can you think gold dust of this guy!"

"He could help us find the treasure," Dom said. "We need to change our thinking. This tree thing. And the half circle. We won't find it in the next park, right? I remember it. No trees in that park. So we need to start thinking about where else it could be. He could help us."

"And he could take the money if we ever find it," Pancho said. "At least he'll want a share. Mr. Kowalski won't get it all back."

"You guys! He's fine. He can help us. He'll help us figure things out."

Pancho's forehead was scrunched. "Look," he told Dom. "I get it." Then he looked at the doc. "But we need to call your grandmother. We have to know if he's for real."

Steph sighed and put her hand out to Dom. "Borrow your phone?"

Dom was sure they weren't going to find out anything they didn't already know, but she had no choice.

"I think I'll go see Roco while you talk," she said. And she left the table.

She had to think about how to handle things. Pancho was not giving Juan Largo a chance. What if Pancho was still stubborn even after Steph's grandmother told them Juan Largo was a babysitter for real? And Juan was right. She had to think of the mission. They needed to find the money. She had to figure out how to win her crew over.

She stepped around the side of the restaurant, toward the kitchen; but she never got there. Through a window she heard Juan Largo's voice.

"They bought the whole thing," he said. "They've given me a name: Juan Largo. That girl thinks she's so smart." The voice stopped for a long second. "It doesn't matter if it's the bad guy in *Treasure Island*! I'm in—don't worry. I'll get the map. We'll be the ones to find the money."

Noooooo! Dom tripped over a hose, making so much noise she figured for sure the villain would find her.

Why didn't she see who he really was?

Why didn't she pay attention to Pancho?

She bolted back to the picnic tables.

She landed, panting, in her seat. "Jim Hawkins and the apple barrel!" she said, hoping they would get what she meant even if she didn't get to finish. "He's a fake! He's trying to get the money."

"Of course he is!" Pancho whisper-yelled. "Steph's grandma didn't send him."

"So—so what do we do?" Steph's voice was trembling, just a little.

"He can't know we know," Pancho whispered more calmly now.

"So we still go to Monroe Park, even though we know that's not it."

"And then we ask him to come to my house to meet my gran!" Steph said. "That will get rid of him!"

Pancho coughed softly. Dom looked toward the restaurant's door.

Juan Largo was coming out carrying a tray with four ice cream cups. Ms. Belle was right behind him with lemonade.

Dom leaned in and whispered, "Just follow my lead at the park. Sleepover tonight . . . at Doc's. We'll figure it out!"

Her crew barely nodded.

Dom whispered one last warning.

"Don'tsayanythingelse." Then she turned to Juan and spoke out loud. "Those look yummy. Thank you!"

After the ice cream, they all went to the kitchen to thank Ms. Belle. Then they headed toward Monroe Park. Roco followed.

Dom was sure smoke was coming out of her ears, but she had to make sure Juan Largo, or whoever he was, didn't know his secret was out. Somehow, she had to keep calm until they could get rid of him.

She marched toward the park where she and Pancho had met Steph. Her crew was close behind her. Juan Largo brought up the rear, but he never let them get out of his sight, or hearing.

9
What Dom Found at Monroe Park

Monroe Park was small. It had a fountain in the middle. Like a wedding cake, with layers of flowing water each higher than the other. In each corner there were beds with bushes and flowers. But just a few steps from the pirate crew, at the entrance from Fifteenth Street, there was a sundial.

If they hadn't been on a mission, Dom would have wanted to dip her feet in the fountain, like Steph was doing the day they found her. Like the blond girl with the baseball cap and the skateboard was doing right now. She was sure Pancho and Steph wanted the same. But they had to find Mr. Kowalski's money. In a hurry. Because Juan Largo or J.L. or whoever he was, was a real villain, and she had to get rid of him as soon as possible. She dropped her bag next to the sundial. Roco lay next to it.

"Nothing much here," Dom said. "Guess we were wrong thinking of parks."

"No, no," Juan said. "You weren't wrong. This is the right park. Here's a sundial. We're looking for a sundial, right?"

Pancho, Steph, and Dom stopped as if they'd run into the boom of the ship's mast. Each looked at the other two. They had talked about parks, and trees, and numbers. True, they had talked about dials. And Rafi had mentioned a sundial. But not in front of Steph. This confirmed her suspicion. There was no way Juan Largo should have known about a sundial.

He got his information from somewhere—or someone—else! It had to be the robbers!

Pancho was the first one to come out of the trance.

"Sundial, mate. Sundial. Shiver my timbers. Yes. There's a sundial."

"You can cut the funny stuff and tell me all that you know," Juan Largo said. "If we put our heads together, we can find it."

Dom's brain whirred. She needed to get rid of Juan. Without him knowing that she was suspicious. AAARGH!

"You know?" Dom said. "You're right. The map Steph showed you? It's not the real map. We don't have that map with us. Of course we don't. We wouldn't want to lose it. And I think you're right. You could help us."

"What are you doing?" Pancho asked, stepping toward her.

"We can't hand over the real map!" Steph said.

Yes! It was working. Pancho and Steph did exactly what she wanted them to do. She raised an eyebrow at Juan Largo. She needed him to think she was on his side.

Dom swept the park with her left arm. "We haven't found anything, right? We have to change tack. Think about something other than trees. And four heads *are* better than three. We'll go home now and meet tomorrow. At the officers' cabin. Two bells, forenoon watch."

A small silence followed.

"I guess," Pancho said. "No trees here for sure."

"And four heads *are* better than three," Steph said.

Pancho huffed and nodded toward Steph. "Let's go. I had plans for tonight anyway."

"Yeah, me too." Steph followed him.

Perfect! Now to put on the finishing touches.

She looked at Juan Largo with her most honest, innocent face. She lowered her voice. "I really don't have the map. Honest. And we have to give it time. Just be patient. If I make them take you in, right now, they'll give me the black spot for sure. *And* you won't get to see it."

"Hrmph," Juan Largo said.

"Anyway." Now Dom's voice was more normal. "Shouldn't you be taking Steph home? Isn't that what your aunt wanted you to do?"

Juan Largo shuffled off to follow Steph and

Pancho. Dom hadn't given him a choice. If he didn't follow Steph, he would give himself away.

✕ ✕ ✕

Dom took a deep breath. She relaxed. A little. She would head home and get her stuff for the sleepover. Maybe even talk to Rafi. They had to figure out a different tack to find the treasure.

She reached down to give Roco a final tummy rub and get her sailor's bag.

And that's when she saw them.

Three trees.

Only three trees.

But three trees on the roof of a building that over-looked the park.

At the end of the *diagonal* of the *sundial.*

She was sure this was the place. The fourth tree was probably on the far side of the roof so she couldn't see it. Or maybe it had died. She had to check it out. And see if they were thirty-seven feet apart. And she had to do it quickly.

She wanted to jump. She wanted to dance. She wished she could run after her mates and tell them.

But she couldn't. She'd have to wait until the sleepover. But she had to check out those trees on the roof right now before Juan Largo returned. And she was sure he would. When she turned, she almost ran into the blond on the skateboard.

"Ooof!" What was it about the girl that was so familiar? Why was she always wherever Dom was?

Dom dodged the girl and took off running. She had to tell someone, but she couldn't reach her crew. Rafi was playing video games with some friends. If she told Mami and Papi, they'd tell her to come straight home and let the police look for Mr. Kowalski's money. Abuela! Abuela would understand. She punched her number.

"I—I—I f-f-found it. I—I—I—th-th-think. Kowalski's money—the money that was stolen—where it could b-b-be," she told her grandmother as she ran.

"Stolen, Dominguita?"

Awww. Now she wished she hadn't called. "Remember, my friends and I are pirates. We're looking for the money someone stole from Mr. Kowalski in 1967."

"That's when I graduated from high school," Abuela said. "I remember. Jake ended up in the hospital after graduation."

"You got it, Abuela! I'm going to get in the building—the building where it is."

"But what if someone sees you?"

Abuela had a sister named Yuyú. "I'll tell them I'm visiting mi tía Yuyú. They won't be able to figure out there's no one there with that name," Dom said.

"Sounds like a plan. Fair winds and all that."

"Already on my way."

10
What Dom Figured Out

The building took up the whole block. She began to walk around it, counting. Turning around every fifteen steps to make sure Juan Largo wasn't following her. She didn't find the building's entrance along the first two sides. All she found was a locked door on Jackson Street. Finally, when she got to the opposite side of the block from where she started—Twenty-Eighth Street—luck was with her. A crescent-moon driveway! The half circle cut out of the rectangle!

Her heart whirled like a waterspout. So hard she had to stop and breathe. Just breathe.

Now she had to get inside.

The entrance was like her building's. Visitors called an apartment, and the people in the apartment could buzz the door open. If a person lived in the apartments, all they had to do was press a code into a keypad. When a lady carrying a lot of packages stepped off a bus, Dom hurried to help her.

And watched.

Pretending not to.

While the woman punched in her code.

Zero-seven-zero-eight.

What luck! Abuela's birthday. It was the code her family used on everything. When the woman disappeared into the elevator, Dom slipped into the building.

The inside was a little fancier than where Dom lived, but not much. And Dom knew her own building backward and forward. She'd been to the roof many times. She punched the button for the top floor—sixteen.

The elevator door opened into a hallway. In front of her, one door was labeled JANITOR'S CLOSET and another was labeled ROOF TERRACE. She tried the one labeled ROOF TERRACE.

It was open!

Yessss! The area to the right of the semicircle had been a sitting area. Sometime. The three trees she saw from the park were planted in pie-shaped planters, each bordered with a short little wall. Like she'd figured, an old rotting stump peeked through reddish weeds in a fourth planter. And the four planters seemed to form a square!

There were benches, tables, and chairs on the "terrace." Broken, dirty, scattered around. They hadn't been used in years. She thought about trying to find out whether the distance between the trees was thirty-seven feet, or steps. But that was hard without a measuring tape. And her steps wouldn't be as long as a robber's. *And* she was in a hurry.

Instead, she pictured the two diagonals meeting. And right there—where she figured they met—she found it: a drain.

She used the dandelion weeder to pry the vent open. And stuck her hand in.

Nothing.

Nothing.

Not that she could reach. The pipe under the drain went off to her right, and she tried to reach in there.

Nothing.

Again.

As far as she could reach.

Okay. That wasn't the worst thing that could have happened. Maybe the keys, or a note, had been at the little x and the actual treasure was still at the big X. That's what Pancho thought, right? That was ten feet north of the little x.

With her compass, Dom found north. And the place where the treasure should be—one of two sets of stairs leading down to short A-shaped sheds in the middle of the square area. To the right of the semi-circle. This had to be it.

She skirted the tumbled-down tables and chairs between her and the shed, went down a few steps, and trembling, put her hand on the knob.

A sound behind her.

She jerked her head around.

Caught!

"Who you? I no see you before." The old man in coveralls had a thick Spanish accent.

Dom breathed a little easier. "Uh, I'm visiting mi tía Yuyú." Dom came out with it as if it were the total truth.

"Niños not allowed up here alone." The man's forehead was scrunched up. It was easy to tell he was upset. "Your tía. Why she not follow rules?"

"*Oh, no, no.* She doesn't know. I told her I was going to the park, but I wanted to check for pirate ships from up here." Dom pulled down her eye patch.

"You a real pirate?"

Dom didn't say yes, but she didn't say no.

"A good pirate?"

Dom wasn't bad, so she nodded.

"You looking for treasure? I know where treasure is." All of a sudden the man was nervous, as if he wanted to take back what he'd just said.

Treasure? Dom's mouth dropped. Had Juan Largo

83

somehow beaten her there? "What treasure?"

"I see the man put a bag in there. He think I don't know, but I see him. I hide, and I see him."

Dom straightened up. "Who? Who did you see? What did he do?" Dom stared at the old man.

"He worked here sometimes. Told me to let him in the building and I did. When I see him hide it, I didn't know it was money. But I watch him. From my room." The man pointed to a little window in the building—the janitor's closet.

"He put the bag in there." He touched the door Dom had been hoping to open. "I saw him, then he saw me."

"Oh no!"

"He told me to guard the bag. It had money in it. He or his brother come get it. If I don't let anyone take the bag, he give me a share. If someone get bag, he tell the police I stole the money. That's what he say. My name is Ben Gonzales. I keep the money."

Wait. Had she heard right?

Ben Gonzales didn't give her a chance to ask. "I keep it safe. I'm janitor. I live here. Room 4A, in the basement. I hid money. No one find it. If some-one come up here, I see in camera. Nobody come. Nobody. Till you. Today."

Dom's heart stopped. Ben Gonzales had just said he still had the treasure.

Ben Gonzales frowned. "You come to get the money? I give it to you. You don't turn me in."

Dom crossed her heart. She had to keep him talking to find out about the money. "I don't take the money, and I don't turn you in."

"Why you come, then?" Ben Gonzales said.

How could she explain the truth? "Ben, that man—the man who hid the money. He's a thief. He took the money from Kowalski's Grocery, in 1967. I want to give it back to Mr. Kowalski."

"Ladrón?"

Dom nodded. "Ladrón. Thief."

Ben took a bit to think about what Dom was saying.

"Maybe he was caught and went to jail," Dom said. "And that's why he never came back to get it."

Ben finally nodded. "No one know where money is. Just me."

"Ben," she said. "Another bad person's trying to get the money now. He's tall and blond and has blue eyes."

"He old?"

Dom shook her head. "Thirteen or fourteen."

"The one that hid it. Him. Tall and blond. I bet he old like me now, though."

"You can't let anyone up here, or tell them about the treasure. No one. You get it?" Dom was afraid Juan Largo could talk the old man into spilling everything.

Ben Gonzales nodded.

"I'm going now. And I'll be back. And I'll make sure no one hurts you. But don't let *anyone* in. Or tell them anything. That blond guy. He's not good people."

"No worry. You no worry."

"Don't talk to him. I'll make sure no one hurts you. I promise."

"You sure? You take care of me?"

How could she let Ben know she wouldn't let him down? She slipped the single lens off her neck and handed it to Ben. "Here. This is my special pirate spyglass. You use it to scout around. You see that bad guy and you hide. Don't even talk to him, right?"

Ben took the squatty lens.

"You go to your tía Yuyú's house now?"

"No, Ben, I have something else I have to do."

"Maybe you'd better look bad guy not coming."

Ben handed the lens back to Dom and motioned to the wall at the edge of the roof.

Dom took it. Stepped to the edge of the wall. She had to get on her tiptoes to see over it. She looked.

"HIDE!"

Juan Largo was about to cross into the park.

Heading toward Roco.

And her sailor's bag.

Which held the real map.

And which she'd left under the sundial in all the excitement.

She handed Ben the lens.

"That's him!" Ben said. "I hide in the furnace room. Nobody find me. You go to Tía Yuyú's house. Nobody find you."

"Uh, uh, uh." Why was it that she got caught every time she lied?

"You go to Tía Yuyú's house. He don't find it. He go away. Then we safe."

She nodded and started out toward the elevator. She couldn't let Ben Gonzales know she'd lied to him. It would be like laughing at him. She didn't have any choice but to pretend to go to her imaginary aunt's house.

Get out of the building.

And call for help.

She had to do it in a hurry.

She punched the down button and pulled on Ben's sleeve. "We'll go down. You go down to your room and stay until I come get you. Hide. Don't talk to that man. That man is bad."

"You come get me?"

"Yes. And I'll take care of you, I promise." She got off on the third floor.

As she got out of the elevator, she was already punching in Rafi's number. This was important enough to interrupt him. She needed Pancho's number from her school directory.

11
What Happened to Dom

Dom found the steps and darted down to the ground floor. She followed the exit signs, opened the door, and stepped out right about the time that her brother answered. She told him about the building. And Ben Gonzales. And the money. And that they couldn't let Juan Largo get it.

As she talked, she walked toward the park, a plan forming in her head.

"What I'll do is pull him away from the building. I know how. It will work."

"Dom . . ."

She had to get everything out, so she didn't let him speak. "What you need to do is come to the building, find Ben Gonzales, and protect him. Maybe you can get him to take the money to the police. But at least, you need to be there so even if Juan Largo gets away from me, he won't be able to get Mr. Kowalski's money. Juan Largo's slick like Long John Silver. He'll talk Ben Gonzales out of his shoes if he wants to."

"Dom . . ."

"I'm getting close now. I'm coming around the corner to the park."

"Dom . . ."

"WHAT?" She didn't have a chance to hear what else her brother would say. Juan Largo was right in front of her. She said the only thing that she could say. "Abuela's birthday!" Then she turned to Juan Largo. Smiling.

"Hey! That was quick! You're just the person I want to see."

Juan Largo didn't look as surprised as she'd expected, but she barreled on.

"I'm on the way to Grant Park. Yesterday the crew wouldn't check the woods when we were there. We looked at a map and it didn't look like there was anything there. But now. Well, now. We've checked the other two parks and ruled them out. So I want to go back and make sure." She took a bearing north and got underway, away from the building and toward Grant Park. "I'd love it if you came with me. You said four heads are better than three, so two heads are definitely better than one." She reached for the sailor bag's strap. "Thanks for bringing my bag. And Roco."

Juan Largo pulled back on the bag. "No problem. I'll carry it for you."

"Oh no, no, no. Really. I can do it." She reached for the strap again. "It's the captain's bag, you know. I ought to carry it."

"But it's the least I can do." Juan put the bag on

his other shoulder. "The captain shouldn't burden herself."

Dom had to give in. If she made a bigger deal of the bag, he might decide to open it right then and there. And he'd find the map. And everything would be over. They were actually walking away from the building. She had to be happy with that much. She'd get the bag back the first chance she had.

They covered a block in silence, Dom getting on the bag side of Juan Largo and trying to figure out in her mind the longest way to get to Grant Park without him getting suspicious.

"So why did you come back?" she finally said. "Steph's gran's not paying you anymore."

"It's a puzzle. I want to solve it. I like you. I want to help you."

Dom was flattered. For about a second. Then she remembered what she'd heard at the Holland House Restaurant. And she remembered *Treasure Island*.

"Hrmph! I think you want the money for yourself. Like Long John Silver. You're just buttering me up."

"Me want the money?" Juan Largo stepped in front of her and stopped—his hands firmly on his hips. As he made that move, Dom's sailor bag slipped off his shoulder.

Quick as a waterspout, Dom grabbed the bag and transferred it to her own shoulder. She dug inside, acting like she did it for Roco. "What do you want, boy? You hungry? I bet you I can find a biscuit in here for you."

Juan was surprised at Dom's move, but she had been so slick that there was nothing he could do. He didn't even try to go for it. She had the bag now. And she was holding it tight under her arm. Her other hand was on the hilt of her dandelion weeder. Just let him try to take that bag away now!

They waited while Roco scarfed up the biscuit, Dom loving every minute that would give her time to get to Ben Gonzales. Even if Juan Largo wasn't crazy about it, they continued on their course to Grant Park.

Now it was his turn.

"So what was that Pancho and ah-boo-ela birthday thing? Some kind of code?"

Was he suspicious? "I was talking to my brother. Abuela means grandmother. Today's her birthday. I wanted to make sure he calls her. And Pancho and Steph need to know I'll be late, but I don't want to talk to them. They'll ask too many questions."

She could tell Juan Largo didn't buy any of what she said, but he didn't call her a liar, either. What he did do was try to turn about. "You're not gonna find anything in Grant Park," he said. "You already went there."

Jump on the yardarm, she had to turn him back.

"No, no, no." Dom moved back to block Juan's way. "We didn't check everything out. We definitely have to go back to Grant Park if you want to see that map tomorrow."

That did it. PHEW! Juan was fuming, but he was heading north again.

Dom figured she'd better explain, in minute detail, how the other two had talked her out of doing a proper investigation at Grant Park. She would take as long as she could. And longer. She needed enough time to get to Ben Gonzales. She talked about Sherlock Holmes.

"I thought you were a pirate, not a detective."

"That's exactly what Pancho said. But we're looking for treasure. Being a detective's a good thing when you're looking for treasure. It's a puzzle. Just like you said."

He certainly couldn't deny that.

Dom was delighted. It was working. She was

reeling him in, slowly, like a huge fish. "It's true." She nodded with gravity. "First you list all your ideas. And you check them out. If they're good, you solve the problem. If they're not good, you rule them out. When you have only one left, even if it doesn't make sense, that's it!"

Juan was still heading in the right direction, so she kept on.

"We decided on three parks. We've ruled out two. Now we have to rule out the third one. Really rule it out. Then if we don't find it at the last park, we have to look at whatever's left."

"The sundial . . ."

"Exactly!" This was going even better than she expected. She was about to land the fish. "The sundial. Tomorrow we tell them we checked all the paths at Grant Park and there was nothing. So the sundial has to be our new clue. Even if it doesn't make sense. They'll buy it. I'm sure. *If* we don't find anything promising at Grant Park."

"That's the craziest thing I've ever heard!"

"Sherlock Holmes always solves the mystery."

Juan Largo stopped, as if striking his sails. "I'm not doing this," he said. "It's the sundial. I know you have that map and it has a sundial."

He tried to reach for the bag, but Dom slipped away from him.

"I don't have a map, and even if I did, I wouldn't give it to you. I have to wait for my crew." She thought of grabbing her dandelion weeder but decided to leave it. She'd probably look ridiculous trying to defend herself from a desperate criminal with a garden tool. She held her bag even closer.

Juan relaxed. "You know it's the sundial," he said again sweetly. "We can tell your crew that we went. We'll check the sundial now, just the two of us. Don't wait till tomorrow."

"I can tell you for sure there's no sundial on our map. You'll see. There's no sundial." She decided to live dangerously. "Is there a sundial on yours?"

"Well . . . yeah," Juan Largo said. Then he looked as if he wanted to swallow his tongue.

Gotcha! "So you *do* have a map."

Juan tried to walk his words back. "I was talking

about yours. I thought your map had a sundial. It has to."

Right. Dom headed north again, in the direction of Grant Park. Juan Largo came back to her like a remora to a shark. Roco followed.

In another block, Juan stopped for the third time.

Thunder! Would he never give up?

"We need to go back," he said. "The money's in the building and I know you went in the building." He steered south and got under way.

Dom followed, trying to find a way to bring him back around. How could Juan Largo know that she went in the building unless he had spies?

He wasn't around when she looked up the dial and saw the trees. He had to have a spy. Skateboard Girl! Blond, tall, following-Dom-everywhere Skateboard Girl! She pulled up the image in her mind and she could see it clearly. Skateboard Girl looked just like Juan. They might even be twins they looked so much alike.

"Of course I went in the building. I was visiting

mi tía Yuyú. She lives on the third floor." Dom pulled out her phone, taking a while to find the picture she wanted. It was her grandmother, not the imaginary Tía Yuyú, but Juan Largo didn't know that. "Sweetest old lady you'll ever know. Now that my abuela is in Florida, she's really lonely. I was so close. I figured I'd stop and see her."

Dom could tell Juan was weighing what she'd said. For a second.

"I don't believe you," he said. "You went to get the money."

Dom decided it was time to hit it head-on. "What if I did? The money's not yours."

"It isn't yours, either."

"It's Mr. Kowalski's, and I'm trying to make sure he gets it."

"What makes you think I'm not?"

"Oh yeah, right!" Dom held on to her dandelion weeder even harder. She didn't like Juan Largo's tone of voice.

"All this *Treasure Island* stuff. You've just been telling stories. All sorts of stories. I don't think you've told the truth the whole time I've been around you. Why should I believe that you'll give the money back to Mr. Kowalski?"

"Because—because he dubbed me a knight. With his . . ." Dom wanted to say with his awesome sword, but that day Mr. Kowalski couldn't find the key for the case with the sword. They'd had to use a metal hook for opening shutters.

Juan snickered. "Dubbed you a knight! Get real!"

"You get real!"

"The money is real. It was a real robbery. And the money needs to go back to Mr. Kowalski," Juan explained.

"See?" Dom said. "That's why I can't believe you! You're just like Long John Silver. Acting like you're so honest . . . like you want exactly what I want."

"But you and Pancho made that up. I'm not Long John Silver! I'm not a character in a book!" Juan yelled.

"Oh yeah? J.L.? Sure. That's your name. John Long? Long John? And your aunt is Auntie Em? That's why I can't believe you. All Long John Silver wanted was to get the money, no matter what!"

Juan Largo raised his empty hands. "Tell me how I'm gonna get your money!"

Dom's fist tightened around her weeder even harder. "If I take you back to the building, you'll take the money."

This time it was Juan Largo's turn to gloat. "So it *is* in the building! I knew it!"

She had blabbed again.

She would have kicked herself and then tried to find a way out of the problem except her cell phone vibrated. Like a sail full of wind.

She pulled away and tried to hide the screen from Juan, but she didn't have to. His cell phone was screaming as furiously as hers.

One text. Two texts. Three texts. More. Dom took off like a ship trying to outrun a storm. "Gotta go," she yelled back at Juan Largo, who'd just put his own phone away and was rushing to follow her.

Juan had longer legs, but Dom was fast. Really fast. They got to the building at the same time, huffing and panting.

When they got to the door, Dom stopped. Should

she let him in? She didn't have a choice. He wouldn't give up and go away. If she wanted to get to the roof of the building, she had to bring the villain with her. She pushed zero-seven-zero-eight. He brushed her aside, headed for the elevator, and pushed the highest number. Dom managed to get in as the elevator doors closed.

12
What the Crew Did When Dom Was with Juan Largo (As Told by Doc)

"Where is he now?" Steph's grandmother asked after Pancho and Steph told her all that had happened.

"He turned around on our way over here. He said his job was done. That he was sure Steph would be safe now." Pancho looked out through lacy curtains. "I was hoping we could follow him, but if we didn't keep coming, he'd know that we know."

"I'm so sorry, but I had no idea. . . . All I said was you guys were having so much fun! You thought you found a real treasure map. But I did say I didn't like you straying so far. Or riding the bus." Steph's gran nodded.

"That's all he needed," Steph said. "He knew about the robbery. He was the one who checked out the *Mundytown Weekly* box. And he checked out the books at the library, looking for the map. Gotta be him. Gran told him we found the map he wanted. And told him about being worried. He made up a story around it."

"He knew some stuff already. And if we'd shown him the real map, he would have run with it and found Kowalski's money." Pancho looked at Steph's grandmother. "At least we can call the beauty shop. Find out where he lives."

Steph agreed. "Then we call the police and they figure out where the loot is."

✕ ✕ ✕

Steph's grandma's shoulders sagged when she hung up the phone. "He's not her nephew. The tall blond boy came into the shop right after I did, and he didn't stay. He never got a haircut."

"So he heard everything."

"And he followed me this morning." Steph punched the kitchen table.

"And we swallowed his story."

"We swallowed it all right."

Steph's gran spoke up. "Someone told him about the robbery. He wasn't alive when it happened."

"We need to call Dom."

Pancho got Dom's number from his mother. They put the call on speakerphone.

But Dom wasn't home.

Rafi told them everything Dom had said. She'd pull Juan Largo away so they could get to Ben Gonzales.

"Rafi . . . the lady in the beauty shop . . . she didn't know the kid. . . ." Steph's gut was rolling. She started again. "Rafi, I think . . . I think we'd better call the police."

Rafi coughed. "Right. I agree. But not just because of that. . . . I found the robber's name.

Back in 1967. It was John Long. I was about to tell her, but the kid showed up and I couldn't. We should call the police."

"Police? Takes too long. And then the sirens . . . ," Steph's gran said. "We'll take my neighbor Captain Finnamin with us. He's retired police. He'll know what to do. Just run, Rafi. We'll meet you there."

"I'm leaving right now."

✕ ✕ ✕

Steph's gran dropped them off and stayed with the car.

"Ugh! We have to wait till someone lets us in," Pancho said when they got to the door by the circular driveway.

"No problem." It was Rafi. He joined the crew and Captain Finnamin and punched zero-seven-zero-eight into the keypad. The door buzzed. "Magic!"

While Steph held the door for the others, a blond girl rushed up.

"May I come in too, please?" she asked. "I've buzzed my aunt three times and she's not answering."

The girl was holding a skateboard and had a baseball cap pulled way down on her face.

Still. There was something familiar about her. Steph was about to ask Pancho to take a look when Rafi elbowed her and pointed to the burly man's flip-flops.

Police, Steph mouthed. *Captain Finnamin.*

Pancho punched the top floor button on the elevator. The minute they opened the door to the rooftop, they saw an arrow, drawn in blue chalk, pointing to the door of one of the two triangular sheds.

Steph, Rafi, and Pancho all looked at one another. Pancho shrugged. He stepped down and pulled on the door handle.

"Yee-haaa!" Ben Gonzales jumped out, waving a broom and a feather duster, his arms whirling like a weather vane.

Before Rafi and the crew could say anything to calm him down, Ben yelled, "Ladrón!" and ran toward the blond-headed girl.

Which was surprising.

Because none of them had realized Skateboard Girl had followed them to the roof.

"You a girl!" Ben Gonzales said.

"Of course I'm a girl," Skateboard Girl said.

"Are you following us?" Steph said. "I thought you were going to your aunt's."

"When you pushed sixteen, I thought I'd come with you. I always like coming up here to look at Mundytown. I'll go down to see her in a minute."

"What's your aunt name?" Ben Gonzales said. "You have a tía Yuyú too?"

"Uh—uh—uh—" Skateboard Girl's eyes got huge. She nodded fast. Really fast.

Rafi put his hand on Ben Gonzales's arm. "Ben," he said.

"How you know my name?"

"Dom. The pirate girl. She told me about you."

"She no have Tía Yuyú. I know. But she take away ladrón. She help me."

"Ben, her name is Dom. She did take away the

ladrón." Rafi points to the rest of the crew. "She told the three of us to come help you."

"That girl, the ladrón, he look like her. He say he take me to police if I tell, and they put me in jail. And she no have Tía Yuyú, either. No Tía Yuyú in the building."

Rafi nodded.

"The pirate girl, she say she take care of me if I don't tell. I don't tell. Not you. Not nobody."

"Dom knows where the money is?" Captain Finnamin asked.

"Pirate Girl not know where money is. Nobody know. Only me. And I not tell."

Captain Finnamin approached Ben Gonzales. "Look here, man, I'm from the police. You and I need to talk."

"Police! I no want police!"

Steph put a hand on Ben's arm. "Pirate girl is on the way. The police will help you."

"Only thing we'll do is go to this corner and talk," Captain Finnamin said. He steered Ben Gonzales

away from the crew, turned up some chairs, and sat down.

Rafi signaled to Pancho and Steph. They huddled by one tree.

Skateboard Girl drifted to another.

It would have been like boxers, getting ready for a fight, except that both corners pulled out their phones.

Rafi: In building. Found BG. Blond skateboard girl here. BG says she's ladrón.

Dom: I know. Juan's sister! OMG!

Skateboard Girl: In building. With Pancho, Steph, and dude named Rafi.

Juan: Dom's brother!

Rafi: Steph brought a cop. In flip-flops. Need to tell him all u found.

Dom: Cop?

Rafi: Steph's neighbor.

Skateboard Girl: Talking about robbery. There's an adult here. I need to tell him.

Juan: Cop?

Skateboard Girl: Can't tell. In shorts and flippies. Best we got.

Rafi: Where U?
Dom: One block.

Skateboard Girl: Where U?
Juan: Can see the building.

Rafi: We need to tell the cop. Tell him everything you told me.
Dom: NOOOOO. STAAAALLL. I want to be there. We need to protect BG!!!!

Skateboard Girl: We need to tell the man. What if they blab?
Juan: STAAALLL. I'll be there in a second.

Rafi and Skateboard Girl looked up from their phones at the same time.

Their eyes locked.

Rafi was the first to start laughing. "Texting with your bro?" he said.

She finally cracked a smile. "Yup. Your sister?"

"Wait, wait," Pancho said. "What's going on?"

"I believe the mystery of Kowalski's robbery is about to be made clear by Long John Silver and Captain Dom."

13

What Happened When They Were Back Together

"I'm Captain Finnamin of the Mundytown Police," the burly man said. "Who wants to go first?"

Juan gave a doubtful look at the man in shorts and flip-flops, but then he began to talk.

"My name is John Long," the blond boy said. "The third. John Long Jr. was our great-uncle. My father named me after his own grandfather, but that also meant he named me after a crook. Our grandfather died three weeks ago." John shifted and reached into a pocket in his pants. "Madison and I were helping our grandma out last weekend—keeping her company—and this is what we found."

Captain Finnamin took the yellowed piece of paper John offered him. "Mmmm." He looked at Dom. "This talks about a park with a sundial and refers to a book at the Mundytown library. *Treasure Island.* It says *that* map has the rest of the information."

"My grandfather never did anything with it, even though his brother begged him," John continued, looking at his feet. "At least that's what my grandmother says. Grandpa was ashamed of what his brother had done."

"Why didn't he turn that piece of paper in?" Rafi asked the question that was in all their heads.

The blond girl looked at Dom. "We don't know a lot. Our grandmother says that at first Grandpa didn't want the police to find the money because it would be worse for his brother."

"But John Long died in prison, years and years ago," Captain Finnamin said. "In some kind of accident, if I remember correctly."

"I know," John said. "He was still young. Maybe Grandpa didn't want people to know about the robbery. It'd have to be in the news if he turned the paper in. And maybe he figured the money was already gone. He didn't even tell our grandma about his brother until a couple of years ago."

"When we showed Grandma the paper," Madison added, "she told us that she wished she could make things right. We decided to try."

"Why didn't you tell us right away?" Dom asked. "We could have really worked together! We wasted so much time!"

"We wanted to be the ones to do it," Madison said.

"I figured if we could find it, we could turn it in," her brother added. "We could talk the police into keeping it quiet. No one would have to know. Our grandma wouldn't be embarrassed. Once I met you, I figured you'd blab. And everyone would know."

Dom was ready to complain that she wouldn't blab, but she really couldn't say that. Not the way she'd been acting. And she also couldn't say the same thing about her brother. Rafi had written an article about them for the *Mundytown Weekly* when they'd saved a little kid. He wanted to get articles in the paper, hoping that maybe, someday, they'd give him a job.

"I won't do anything for the paper," Rafi said. "There are a ton of other adventures to write about. But I will write something for our abuela. She loves to hear about Dom's adventures. I'll change all the names."

"And I'm not a cop anymore," Captain Finnamin said. "I'm retired. And the case is closed. I'll let the precinct know, but so long as Mr. Kowalski gets the money, no one else needs to know."

14

What Happened at the Pizza Party

"**W**e've been trying to find this money since 1967," Captain Finnamin said when they all met at Steph's grandmother's for pizza and chocolate chip cookies.

Ben Gonzales walked over, and John and Madison brought their grandmother. Rafi came to get the whole scoop for Abuela. And Mr. Kowalski and his wife were there to get their money. Roco had stayed. He loved pizza.

The three pirates told the story in great detail so

that Rafi could get it down. They left off when Dom stepped out the door of Ben's building.

That's when Ben Gonzales took over. He figured Dom had made up her tía Yuyú. He watched the cameras and saw her leave and pull the ladrón away from the building.

Ben was sure they'd come back. So he remembered *Treasure Island* and drew the arrow with blue chalk to let Dom know where he was. While he looked for something good with which to help Dom, he saw the crew, Rafi, and the ladrón in the lobby's camera. He grabbed the only things he had in the janitor's closet. But with only that, he figured he had to look wild when he came out to surprise them and catch them. So he could protect Dom.

Madison talked about hearing Dom at Yuca, Yuca, and she knew exactly what map Dom was talking about. She tailed Dom and her crew from the restaurant. She and John followed them to the first park. From there they split up. John was in charge of Steph and Pancho. Madison was in charge of Dom. The next day she hovered around in case any of the "pirates" strayed away from John. She and John texted and talked. That's how John knew Dom had found the building.

Mr. Kowalski was happy that the money had been found.

"It was always one of those things that you wondered about," he said. "Insurance covered the robbery, and I knew the robber was behind bars, so justice had been done. But I always wondered where that money was."

"Well, now you know," Dom said. "Thanks to Ben Gonzales, not a penny is missing."

Mr. Kowalski looked out the window for a long while. He took a swig of soda. "I have to turn the money in to the insurance company," he said, and then he looked at Ben Gonzales. "Someone as honest as you, I'd be happy to have you come work for me. I have an apartment over my shop you're welcome to have. It has windows, and its own bathroom, and a kitchen. Better than a room in the basement. You can help me at night when you can, and I'll pay you. And you can still work at the building all you need."

"Split my sides," Dom said. "That's the most—most"—she had to find a good pirate word—"the most gold dust thing I've ever heard. Jump on the yardarm if it isn't."

"What a story!" Rafi said. Dom could tell he was itching to tell the world.

"You know," she told John and Madison. "Maybe he doesn't have to put any names in the story. It's been such a long time, no one would know it had anything to do with your family."

John Long shook his head. "All they have to do is google Kowalski's robbery and they'd find out."

Dom raised an eyebrow at John Long. "They didn't have internet back then, and the only newspaper issue that carried it mysteriously disappeared."

"Wait," the twins' grandmother said. "What are you talking about?"

Madison stood behind her grandmother. "We don't want you to be embarrassed if this comes out."

"Embarrassed? Embarrassed because my grandchildren did the right thing? Never! Tell the world! I'm as proud as can be."

Everyone finished their pizza, and they were all ready to leave when John approached Dom. "I guess you're unhappy you didn't catch Long John Silver," he told her. He had a half-snarky look on his face.

"Unhappy? Unhappy that our adventure turned out exactly like *Treasure Island*? Never! Long John Silver got away, and Juan Largo got away. Nothing wrong with that!"

✕ ✕ ✕

Rafi wrote his story for the *Weekly*, and after reading it, lots of folks offered to help Ben.

The crew and the twins gathered what they offered and helped Ben make a cozy new home above Kowalski's store.

"That's the way you get things done," Pancho said when they were finished. "One for all and all for one!"

Dom and Steph punched the air. It sounded like a good idea.

Captain Dom's Nautical Glossary

boom: The horizontal beam of wood, attached to the mast, that holds the foot of the sail. The boom swings. By moving the boom, the sailors change the position of the sail and change the direction of the ship.

changing tack: Changing direction.

mast: The vertical beam of wood that rises from the deck of a ship. It serves to hold the sheets (ropes), which haul the sails up and down. The tippy-top of sails are pulled up the mast by ropes on pulleys.

remora: Fish that attach themselves to sharks and eat their crumbs.

sail full of wind: A ship moves when the wind fills its sails. Captains change directions by changing the position of the sails and changing the rudder by turning the wheel. When a sail is really full of wind, the sail, the boom, and the rudder might vibrate.

striking sails: Bringing down the sails to stop the ship.

take a heading: Figure out which way to go.

turn about: A way of saying turn, by using an extra word. Even fancier: come about.

underway: Another way of saying moving, going, or sailing.

waterspout: A churning circle of water that happens when wind whirls itself into a column or funnel reaching from the bottom of a cloud to the surface of the water.

weighing anchor: Lifting the anchor out of the water so that the ship can start moving. "Anchors aweigh" means that the anchors have been shipped (are inside the ship) and the boat can start moving.

yardarm: The end of a beam that holds the upper end of a square sail.

Captain Dom's Treasure **sayings:**

Jump from the yardarm

Yo, ho, ho, and a bottle of pop

These sayings have been modified from the original *Treasure Island* text.

Author's Note

Captain Dom's Treasure is similar to Robert Louis Stevenson's book *Treasure Island.* Stevenson's book was published as a book in 1883. It was about Jim Hawkins, a young boy who found a real treasure map in his family's inn. The treasure had been buried by the infamous Captain Flint. Flint's crew knew of the treasure and were itching to get their hands on it.

Jim gave the map to two trusted men—the doctor and the squire of his town. The squire hired out a ship, and they were ready to search for the treasure. But like Dom, the squire blabbed. Some of Captain Flint's pirates heard him and signed up to go on the trip. What they planned to do was kill Jim, the doctor, the squire, and the captain of the ship they'd hired. Instead, Jim overheard Long John Silver, while napping in an apple barrel, like Dom overheard J.L./Juan Largo.

In one chapter, Jim left his mates, like Dom. The doc in *Treasure Island* narrated the story when Jim wasn't around, like in chapter twelve of this book.

Long John Silver, like J.L., was a charmer. He flattered Jim Hawkins and the squire and got them to believe he had good intentions.

In the end, Jim found Ben Gunn—a man who'd been marooned by pirates on Treasure Island. Ben Gunn found the treasure, and like Ben Gonzales, didn't want it for himself. Jim had many misadventures, but his friends, including Ben Gunn, saved Jim.

Although Long John Silver should have been turned over to be jailed, no one minded when he took a small portion of the treasure and escaped. Even though Long John wasn't always good, no one had wanted to make him pay. That's why Dom was happy with the ending of her pirate adventure.

Acknowledgments

I am indebted to Robert Louis Stevenson for writing *Treasure Island*. It was a fun book on which to base *Captain Dom's Treasure*. Most importantly, he gave me endless hours of virtual adventures the many times I read his book as a kid.

Dominguita and I have a lot in common. My thanks as always to my critique partners, whose wise counsel and nurturing are priceless to me. To Natalie Lakosil, my agent: Thank you for having my back. The editing team at Simon & Schuster and Aladdin continues to make my work shine. But Aly Heller, my superstar editor, let me find the true ending to this story, and she has my undying gratitude.

Lou Jennings, every word I write is because you're with me.

Turn the page for a sneak peek at Dominguita's next adventure!

The Library Book

Dominguita Melendez wore a family heirloom—her grandmother's Pamela hat. She doffed the wide-brimmed floppy purple hat when she reached the librarian.

"Musketeer?" Mrs. Booker peered over her reading glasses to look at Dom. "Is that your next adventure?"

Dom decided to use Musketeer words. "Forsooth!

How'd you guess?" she said. "My hat doesn't even have a feather!"

"Forsooth, indeed. You reserved *The Three Musketeers* last night—dead giveaway." The librarian reached behind her for the book. "Besides, not too many people come into the library wearing a wide-brimmed purple velvet hat, with or without feathers."

"Good point. We'll study the book carefully tonight. We'll be ready for an adventure this weekend."

"You're missing the rest of your crew."

"Pancho had a dentist appointment after school. Steph is at the leg doctor—she's getting a smaller brace. I'm meeting them later. And we already know a lot about the Musketeers. About rescuing the queen's diamonds and all the duels. But we want to refresh our memories. Need to make sure we get our Musketeer talk down pat."

"So you're going with three?"

Dom knew that *The Three Musketeers* was not just about *three* Musketeers. They had a friend. She shrugged. "It doesn't really matter, right?"

"Not at all," the librarian agreed.

"Jim Hawkins was the main character in *Treasure Island*, and none of us decided to be him."

"And you could always change your mind later."

"Yeah. And my brother Rafi's always wanting to join in. He loves *The Three Musketeers* too." Dom leaned in close to the librarian. "He's still writing about us for our abuela, you know."

Mrs. Booker smiled. "Can't wait to read the newest adventure."

Dom put her hat back on. "I'm on the way to Fuentes Salvage to get our equipment. We're meeting tonight to make our plans. We'll bring the book back soon."

"No rush. You have three weeks."

With that, Dom was off.